★ PAWTRIOT ★ DOGS

EVERYTHING'S BIGGER IN TEXAS

by Samuel P. Fortsch
illustrated by Manuel Gutierrez

GROSSET & DUNLAP

I dedicate this book to the brave men and women
of the US Armed Forces. And to my siblings for
their endless love and support—SPF

In memory of Copito, Colita, Toby, Nuky, Flavor, Hermes,
Orson, Jay Boy, and John Fitzgerald Tinta—MG

GROSSET & DUNLAP
An Imprint of Penguin Random House LLC, New York

Photo credit: cover: (paper background): darkbird77/iStock/Getty Images Plus

Text copyright © 2020 by Samuel P. Fortsch. Illustrations copyright © 2020 by
Penguin Random House LLC. All rights reserved. Published by Grosset & Dunlap, an imprint of
Penguin Random House LLC, New York. GROSSET & DUNLAP is a registered trademark of
Penguin Random House LLC. Printed in the USA.

Visit us online at www.penguinrandomhouse.com.

Library of Congress Control Number: 2020024602

ISBN 9780593222348   10 9 8 7 6 5 4 3 2 1

CHAPTER 1
HOOAH!

Location: The Sanctuary: Washington, DC, United States
Date: 10MAR21
Time: 1800 hours

Welcome back, soldier!

I'm glad to see you reenlisted. A lot has happened since we saved the Sanctuary, so let me *debrief* you. That's Army-talk for . . . that's right! I'm glad you remembered.

Winter is coming to an end and the Pawtriots couldn't be happier. Morale is sky-high and we're adding new recruits to our ranks. Dogs, cats, snakes, and birds are arriving every day and they all ask me the same thing: "How can we help?!"

There are so many new animals that we set up a boot camp, right here at the Sanctuary. It's a nine-week program that turns civilians into soldiers. It's like summer camp but with lots of marching and even more push-ups!

After we took down Mr. Mocoso, we knew it was our duty to help others in need—beyond the animals in the Sanctuary. So, we've been using pigeons and other birds to relay messages from all over the country. Calls for help have been pouring in for the past six months.

Penny is always pushing us to go out on missions and do good deeds for the community. "Our community," as she says. But we have to prioritize. We can't help everyone. There just isn't enough time in the day.

I caught her sneaking out the other night to help a pigeon that had some gum stuck on his wings. It was the right thing to do, but it's risky to go off on your own. As leader, it's important for me to know where everyone is at all times. She can't just sneak *outside the wire* whenever she wants to. That's Army-talk for "going out on missions."

We call the Sanctuary "the TOC" now. It sounds like *tock* as in ticktock, and it's short for Tactical Operations Center. The TOC is our command post and it's where we plan our missions. Morgan and Sawyer, the rabbit and ferret, got hurt in a training exercise the other day, so they've been running the TOC when the rest of us are out on missions. They're okay now, but they need time to recover from their injuries. Still, there's an upside to having them stay behind. It's always good to have capable leaders stay in the rear with the gear and make sure things at home run smoothly.

We've even established a chain of command:

Enlisted Paws Identification Card

Sergeant First Class . . . . Rico
Staff Sergeant . . . . Penny
Sergeant . . . . Franny
Specialist . . . . Brick
Specialist . . . . Smithers
Corporal . . . . Sawyer
Corporal . . . . Morgan

Your rank is a badge of leadership and it determines your level of responsibility within your unit.

And we even wrote out our mission statement: "The Pawtriots will provide safety and security to all animals in need."

It's very important to establish a unit's purpose. It helps keep everyone focused on achieving goals and completing missions. Soldiers love knowing that what they're doing is for a good reason.

Time: 2100 hours

I had planned to lead a quick night-op perimeter check at the TOC with the Pawtriots tonight. But the wind is howling and snow is falling fast, so it might be a better idea to conduct classroom training instead. It's not exactly everyone's favorite thing to do, and it's definitely not mine!

Still, I know it's important to do this type of training. Simon, the marmoset who helped us locate the will in Mr. Mocoso's mansion, snuck out of the zoo to join our cause. He's been teaching everyone how to effectively communicate in silence using only hand and arm signals. It takes practice, but I'm confident everyone will learn quickly.

Brick moseys over to me, holding a clipboard with a list on it.

"Is everyone here?" I ask.

Brick scans the list. "Everyone but Penny," he says.

I scan the room. He's right, Penny's not here. She must have snuck out . . . again.

I softly whistle to Franny and Smithers and signal for Simon to "come here."

"Everything okay, Rico?" asks Franny.

"Penny snuck out," says Brick, shaking his head from side to side.

"Again? And in this weather? Are you kidding?" asks Franny.

"Ssseriousssly ill-advisssed," says Smithers.

I know Penny is out there trying to help other animals, but in this blizzard she may be the one who ends up needing help.

I motion to the group to "follow me" and lead Brick, Smithers, Franny, and Simon outside into the snow.

The snow is falling so fast that I can barely see, but we're prepared. We've got these super high-speed goggles. *High-speed*—that's Army-talk for "cool." They're meant to keep our eyes protected and vision clear, but with the wind whipping snow right into our faces, it's hard to maintain a clear line of sight.

"Can anybody see her?" I ask.

"I can barely sssee anything," says Smithers.

"*Oi!* And it's freezing out here," says Brick.

I want to let everyone go inside and get warm, but I just can't. Don't get me wrong; I'm freezing my tail off out here, too. But once you start taking the easy road, it's almost impossible to ever take the hard one.

Suddenly there's a *thud*, and the snow crunches behind me. I spin around to try to figure out where the sound is coming from.

"What was that?" asks Franny.

"Spread out! It could be Penny," I say.

And suddenly, I hear a voice call out, "Help!"

It sounds like Penny, so I quickly scan from side to side, but I can't see where she is.

Then there's another *thud*. The crunching sound is much louder this time.

Through the blustery blizzard, I spot Simon waving his arms frantically as if trying to flag me down. I can see movement just beyond him, but I can't quite make out *what* or *who* the movement is. So I wipe the snow off my goggles to get a clearer look.

"Three o'clock!" I call out so the Pawtriots know which way to look. In Army-talk that's a directional clock position for "to the right."

I trudge through the powdery snow toward Simon, Penny, and a mystery dog. Snow keeps getting stuck in my wheel, but I can see another dog with Penny who is covered in snow and has ice clinging to its whiskers, so I need to keep moving until I reach them.

"I found her in the alleyway. She wasn't moving," Penny says to me.

Instinctively, I grab the dog by the scruff of its neck and drag it toward the TOC, bringing it into safety and warmth. But I worry this pooch might already be frozen to death.

7

CHAPTER 2
GREETINGS FROM TEXAS

Location: The Pawtriots TOC
Date: 10MAR21
Time: 2130 hours

We barge into the TOC, swinging the doors wide open, letting the cold air and snow in. The new recruits are alarmed by the commotion and huddle around us and the mystery dog, asking me lots of questions: "Who's that?" "What's going on, Rico?"

I help Franny and Morgan brush the cold, wet snow off the mystery dog, uncovering wavy, creamy yellow fur. She's a golden retriever. Her eyes are closed and she's lying on the floor, but I can see her chest rising and falling.

"She's alive!" I holler.

The new privates are hovering a little too close, so Brick stands between us and them and puffs out his chest.

"*Oi!* Back up!" Brick hollers, sending all the privates scampering.

The golden retriever adjusts her eyes to the bright lights.

"Sanctuary. Rico . . . Sergeant Rico," mutters the golden.

Penny looks confused and starts to do the "tilt," and then looks over at me. I've never seen this dog in my life, so I'm just as confused as she is.

"I'm looking for Sergeant Rico," the golden says.

Before I can get a word in, the golden passes out.

"Quickly! Get her some blankets," I say.

Smithers drags over a blanket and drapes it on the golden's body. I watch as something catches Smithers's eye.

"What'sss thisss?" he says as he retrieves a rolled-up piece of paper from under the golden's white leather collar that has a big shiny "D" pendant on it.

Smithers hands the paper to me, and all the animals quickly crowd around. I can feel Penny's breath tickling my ear as I unroll the paper and read the message out loud.

DEAR DAISY,
WE HAVE YOUR PRECIOUS LITTLE PUPPIES. IF YOU WANT TO SEE THEM AGAIN, YOU'll LISTEN, AND YOU'll LISTEN GOOD. HEAD NORTHEAST AND KEEP WALKING UNTIL YOU GET TO SANCTUARY AND YOU FIND THOSE NO-GOOD PAWTRIOTS AND THEIR NO-GOOD LEADER, SERGEANT RICO. BRING THEM HERE TO TEXAS AND MEET US AT THE ABANDONED MINE. DON'T THINK. JUST DO IT. YOU'VE GOT ONE WEEK TO BRING ME RICO AND THE PAWTRIOTS. YOU CANNOT GET YOUR PUPPIES BACK WITHOUT THEM. BETTER DOUBLE-TIME... THE CLOCK STARTS NOW!
—DAGR & THE SEVEN POOCHES GANG

I put the note down and can see the golden is awake.

"Is it really you?" the golden asks as she slowly starts to come out of her daze. She looks at my face as if she's drawing from her memory. Her voice has a soft twang to it. Like a southern accent.

I don't have any idea what she's talking about, so I let her continue.

"It is you. I saw your article in the newspaper. Oh, sweet Southern sun, I never thought I'd make it!" she says.

"Who are you? Where'd you come from?" I ask.

"My manners must have blown away with the wind. My name's Daisy, and I've come all the way from Texas with an urgent message from Dagr, the leader of the Seven Pooches Gang."

"We found your note," I say.

"Are you in the Seven Pooches Gang?" asks Penny.

"Oh, heavens no! I want nothing to do with Dagr and all of his wicked ways. He has my puppies. I had no choice but to do what the note said," says Daisy.

Penny eyes Daisy with even more suspicion. "No one *has* to do anything if they don't want to."

"When Dagr tells you to do something, you do it. No questions asked. He's the meanest, nastiest dog you'll ever meet. He and his gang have been terrorizing my hometown for years, and now they've got my puppies!" says Daisy.

I appreciate Penny being skeptical, but sometimes you have to trust your instincts. And my gut says that this golden is friend, not foe.

"When did you get that ransom note?" I ask.

"Six days ago," says Daisy as she wipes tears off her cheek.

"That means we have less than twenty-four hours to get to the abandoned mine," I say.

I watch as Smithers pulls out a map and searches for the location of the abandoned mine.

"*Oi!* Texas is far out of my jurisdiction . . . our jurisdiction," says Brick.

Penny chimes in, "That's not the point, Brick. The Pawtriots will go anywhere to help animals in need, but if it took Daisy six days to get here, then how are we supposed to get there in less than one?!"

I take a moment to think about the mission. Penny and Brick are right: This *is* a daunting task. We're well over two thousand *klicks* away from the drop site. *Klick*—that's Army-talk for "kilometer."

And not only that, but we could very well be walking right into a trap. On the other paw, I can't turn my back on this task. It's our duty to help those in need—that's the Pawtriots' mission statement after all.

I look down at my wheel and think about Kris and Chaps. Kris was my former handler in the Army; she taught me everything. She was there when I lost my leg in the explosion. That was the last day I ever saw her.

And Chaps was the most courageous dog I've ever met. He was the one who sacrificed his life so I could live. He gave me his wheel. I wonder what they would do if they were here. "No guts, no glory"—that's what Kris used to say to me right before a dangerous mission.

I make my way over to the window and whisper a message to one of our carrier pigeons. "Fly fast," I tell her.

I turn back to the group. "All right now, listen up, Pawtriots. I want this mission to go smoothly and by the numbers."

"Rico, give me a break! The fastest dog on Earth

couldn't run there in time," says Penny.

"You're right. But I never said anything about running."

Franny jumps in. "So what exactly did you have in mind?"

"We're going to sneak onto Joint Base Andrews and catch a plane ride to Texas," I say.

Daisy looks up at Penny. "Is he serious?" she says.

"Oh, he's serious . . . seriously out of his mind!" says Penny as she gives me the "tilt."

"Penny, just hear me out—" I say, but she cuts me off.

"No, you hear *me* out. We have problems right here . . . in *our* community. I'm very sorry, Daisy. It's just too far away."

Daisy stands up and shakes the blanket off of her.

"Please, I'm begging y'all to help me get my puppies back! When Dagr gave me that note, I didn't stop running. I ran until my paws went numb and then I ran some more. I jumped on moving trains and swam across rivers. Don't tell me that was all for nothing. What would you do if they were your puppies?"

Penny shakes her head from side to side and then looks at me. "I don't like the way any of this sounds, Rico."

All eyes are on me.

Everyone is waiting for me to make a command decision. As a leader, you have to be resolute. You're either in or you're out. Not everybody's going to agree with every move you make, but you have to trust yourself and your decision. I take a long, deep breath. Then I start handing out marching orders to the Pawtriots.

"Listen up, privates! You are to follow Morgan's and Sawyer's orders while we're in Texas. *Hooah?*" I ask.

All the privates respond in unison: *"HOOAH!"*

I turn to Morgan and Sawyer. "I want them battle ready by the time we return. Should be no more than one week. Are you tracking?" I ask.

"Tracking," they both say.

I look at the rest of the Pawtriots who will be joining me on this southbound mission. "Franny,

Smithers, Simon, Brick, Penny, and Daisy, I need you all ready and mobile. We've got a plane to catch!" I say. "I want everyone to get some quick shut-eye and rest up before our mission."

CHAPTER 3
WHEELS UP

Location: Joint Base Andrews
Date: 11MAR21
Time: 0630 hours

We've got less than twenty-four hours to reach the abandoned mine.

The cold wind is biting, and the sun hasn't started to rise, so we use the darkness to cover our movements. We've got to move quickly. Every minute that Daisy's puppies are in danger is a minute too long. We're about a klick away from the runway, and the plow trucks are almost done clearing off the snow. I'd guess we have less than thirty *mikes* before our ride leaves without us. *Mikes* is Army-talk for "minutes."

I look out into the distance and see the carrier pigeon I sent out earlier flying toward us. She lands on Brick's head and shakes the snow off her feathers.

"I have a message from your Air Force buddy who works on this base. He got word to his brother Lindy at E. F. Dunes Air Force Base in Texas, just south of Corpus Christi. He says he'll be waiting there to help sneak you off the plane," says the pigeon.

"Tracking all. Great work," I tell the pigeon before it flies back to the TOC.

"Daisy, can I have a word with you?" I ask her.

Daisy trudges through the snow and stands in front of me. "Listen, I know you're not used to troop movements and tactics," I say.

"Nope, not in the slightest," says Daisy. "But I was a competition dog, so if you need me to run quick, jump far, or swim fast, well, I'm your girl," she says with a smile.

"All I need you to do is to *not* give away our position. Just watch your *noise and light discipline*. That's Army-talk for 'be quiet and no flashlights,'" I say.

"Anything for my puppies!" she says.

"Great. Let's roll out," I tell her.

We make our way across a long, snow-covered field. The snow is wet and makes for tough work, especially with my wheel. I'm soaked, but I can't let that stop me. We've got a mission to do, and I have a creed to live by—the Soldier's Creed—and it taught me: *I will never quit.*

I scan my surroundings to figure out how to proceed with this mission. I see there is a long chain-link fence lining the entire perimeter of the base's runway. On top of the fence is barbed wire, so we can't just climb over.

"How are we going to get through?" asks Daisy.

Franny chuckles and gives me a wink. We watch as Franny uses her teeth to gnaw through the chain-link fence while Penny and Smithers pull it apart to make a hole.

Daisy is clearly impressed, and says, "Y'all are perfect for this mission!"

With the hole big enough, we squeeze through the fence to keep moving.

Then Penny stops and points to the runway. "Look! Over there!"

I follow her paw and ahead I see it: a massive C-5 Galaxy—that's a big plane! A high-wing military transport aircraft to be exact.

"That bad boy is our ticket to Texas," I say to Penny as the C-5 makes its final preparations before takeoff.

"I sssure hope thisss plane hasss heat!" Smithers cries out.

"*Oi!* Stop whining. You're making the Pawtriots look weak," Brick says as he motions to Daisy.

"*Lock it up,*" I grunt softly. That's Army-talk for "be quiet!"

I take a moment to survey the situation.

There's a long stretch of runway we're going to have to get across undetected. We're trespassing on US government property, and if we get caught, they'll detain us, and this mission will be over before it even started. In the Army we called this type of obstacle an *LDA*. It stands for "linear danger area," and we're instructed to avoid these situations at all costs because they leave your unit exposed and vulnerable. But right now, it's our only option.

I signal for Simon to go first. I watch as he sneaks across the runway without getting spotted, so I signal to the others and tell them to rally on me. "Pawtriots, we have to *double-time* across this LDA." Double-time is Army-talk for "hurry up."

"So what are we waiting for?" Daisy whispers to me.

I point to Simon, who's signaling to "hold" as a plow truck makes another pass down the runway to clear the snow. "Get ready to move out," I say.

Then I point to the plane's cargo door. "That's where we get on. Everybody tracking?"

They all nod.

The plow truck passes by and throws thick wet snow high into the air. "Let's move!" I call out to the Pawtriots.

We race across the runway as fast as we can, rushing for the cargo door before it closes. I've got my eyes on the path ahead but can sense movement to the side. I turn quickly and see another plow truck.

"It's coming right for us!" Penny calls out. "Brick, go faster!"

"*Oi!* You know this is top speed!" he barks back.

We keep sprinting for the cargo door, trying to dodge both plow trucks. Then, suddenly, the second plow truck lumbers by and sends a massive wall of snow high up into the air and right in our direction.

I quickly scan the area. "Where is Daisy? I can't see her!" I ask frantically.

I can feel the ground shake and rumble as the plane's massive engines begin to throttle. I watch as the cargo door begins to close. I know time is running out before the plane leaves.

"Get everyone on that plane!" I call out to Penny and Brick.

But I still can't find Daisy. The snow is coming down fast, and the plane's engines are sending snowdrifts across the tarmac. I can barely see a thing. My eyes are practically useless, so I close them and focus all my attention to my nose. I breathe in and out quickly, lowering my nose to the ground.

I've got a scent! My ears perk up, and I start clearing the snow in front of me. I can see Daisy's fur, so I dig even faster. I clear out all the snow around her, but she doesn't move.

I grab her by the collar and start pulling her toward the plane.

"Fassster!" shouts Smithers from inside the plane.

"Hurry! The door's closing!" says Franny.

I'm pulling as hard as I can, but my wheel is slipping on the snow and ice. This would never have happened if I still had my leg, but I keep reminding myself: *I will never quit.*

I keep pulling Daisy. We're almost to the cargo door when a light flashes directly onto us. But it's not coming from the control tower. It's the plow truck's headlights, and it's coming right for us.

"Daisy! Wake up!" I shout as I nudge her again and again with my snout. But it's too late. I lie down on top of her to shield her body from the truck, and I brace for impact.

"*Oi!* And you all thought I couldn't run fast!" Brick says with a hearty laugh.

I'm a bit dazed, but aware enough to know that was no plow that hit us. It was Brick!

"Snap out of it, Rico. Let's move!" Penny shouts as she helps Brick back onto his feet.

Daisy is startled awake from the impact, and I have her lean on me as we lumber across the runway.

"Hurry!" Franny calls out as she helps us up into the plane just moments before the cargo door closes.

"We made it!" Daisy cheers as we all catch our breath inside the shelter of the plane, safe from the elements.

I feel the plane pick up speed as it barrels down the runway. The engines spin faster and faster, and then the nose of the plane lifts off and the wheels come up. I look out the window at the snow-covered ground, and think to myself, *there's no turning back now.*

CHAPTER 4
PERFECTLY GOOD AIRPLANE

Location: 20,000 feet ASL (Above Sea Level)
Date: 11MAR21
Time: 1000 hours

I almost forgot how loud it is inside these big military planes—almost. I should be getting some shut-eye, but I can't stop thinking about what lies ahead. *Who is this Dagr dog? What does he want with me and the Pawtriots? What does he have against us?*

One thing I do know is that I have to trust myself and my soldier's instinct. I made a command decision to go on this mission. I need to be *all in*. If I'm not, then the rest of the Pawtriots certainly won't be.

I try to let my mind wander and think about simpler times . . . when I was in the Army . . . when I was just a recruit . . . when suddenly, turbulence jolts me from my thoughts. Penny is the first to wake up. She peeks over and notices I'm awake. She knows I'm feeling off. She can always sense my uncertainty.

Penny rubs her eyes and lazily stretches out. Then she saunters over to me and says, "We should probably wake them up."

She's right. The plane is starting to descend, and we'll be landing soon.

"And go over the plan again," Penny says through a yawn.

"Roger that. Pawtriots, on your feet," I say.

Everyone is slow to get up and still half asleep.

They gather around me in a huddle so I can debrief them. They know the drop location and when we're supposed to meet Dagr. Daisy keeps muttering the location under her breath so she won't forget. But Penny's right. Everyone should know the plan. Inside and out. Down to your lowest rank. And just because you're low in rank doesn't mean you're not important.

"The Pawtriots are present and . . . ," Penny stops herself and then looks around. "Wait, where's Brick?"

I look over and see Brick is still *ten toes up*. That's Army-talk for "sleeping on your back."

"I'll wake him up," says Franny.

"Thisss ssshould be interesssssting," says Smithers with a grin.

Franny goes over to Brick and gently nudges him. Brick doesn't even flinch.

"Pull his eyelids back," says Penny.

Just as Franny climbs up onto him to grab his eyelids, the plane rumbles as we descend through some severe turbulence. She loses her footing and falls forward. She is about to hit the floor when she grabs onto a lever sticking up out of the floor nearby.

"Close one," says Franny.

But then a red light starts spinning and a siren begins to wail. We all freeze and look at one another.

We're all unsure what just happened and what we should do next.

I look over at Simon, who is motioning at the lock on the door, which is now unlocked. Before I can react, the cargo door begins to open, sending cold air rushing into the plane.

"*Oi!* What'd you do?!" shouts Brick.

"Nothing, I mean . . . I didn't mean to touch it! I was falling," says Franny.

"Push that lever back into place!" I howl.

I watch as Franny pushes with all her might. "It won't budge," she says.

We all instinctively charge forward and push on the lever with Franny, but it doesn't make a difference. It's not going back into place.

As the cargo door continues to open, more cold, wet air rushes in, lowering the air pressure inside. I can feel the plane go into a steep dive, lifting me and the Pawtriots off our feet. I know the pilots are trying to land this thing quickly to bring the plane to a breathable altitude.

"Grab on!" shouts Penny as she points to a wooden crate wrapped in cargo net. I check to make sure everyone is secure. I know these crates are equipped with parachutes and rip cords, so I get a good grip on it to secure myself.

But then the turbulence picks up and bounces the plane around even more. I look over at one of the straps holding the crate in place; it's buckling and bending.

All I hear is a loud *SNAP*, and then we're sliding out of the back of a perfectly good airplane.

"Hold on!" I howl.

The crate jostles from side to side and then drops out of the back of the plane. We're falling through the sky like a rock, hurtling toward the Earth and running out of time. I realize that I have to do something, and I have to act now.

I know I need to find the rip cord handle and yank it open. I've seen Kris pull it countless times. The crate is tumbling end over end, and my grip on it is loosening, so I have to make sure every move I make is deliberate. I need "*three points of contact.*" That's Army-talk for "keeping hands and feet in contact with the surface at all times." It's proving to be a little difficult with a wheel for a leg.

"Hurry, Rico!" shouts Penny as she points to the massive river below us.

"Oh my, what did I get myself into?" says Daisy.

I look below me and all I see is water. It looks like we're going to crash right into a river, unless I can find this rip cord.

We hit the water—*hard*. But not as hard as we would have had I not found the rip cord.

The crate broke our fall, but it also broke into dozens of pieces upon impact. We all scrambled to grab any piece of wood we could find to use as a flotation device.

Now we're holding on for our lives as the rushing current of the river carries us downstream. I'm panting hard as I try to catch my breath above the water.

But after about one hundred meters, the current slows into a lazy drift and I can finally breathe a bit better than before.

I look around to account for all the Pawtriots. With a big smile on my face I howl, "That was a close one!"

But as I look at all their faces, I see I'm the only one smiling.

"Waterfall!" shouts Penny. I turn back around and realize we're heading right for the edge.

"Quick! Swim for the banks!" I shout.

Smithers races ahead of us, wrapping his body around a dead tree branch that's protruding through the rapids.

"Ssswim to me!" says Smithers.

I see Daisy, Penny, and Brick angle their bodies toward the branch and swim quickly toward Smithers, who reaches out to grab them.

"Come on, guys! Swim to us!" shouts Penny.

I want to make sure the other Pawtriots are safe before I swim to safety, but my wheel is weighing me down. I watch as Simon surfs by me on a piece of broken wood and safely crash lands into the riverbank.

I spot Franny struggling to keep her head above water.

"Franny!" I howl.

I'm swimming as hard as I can, but the rapids are too strong. I'm not going to be able to help, especially since I can barely help myself. I'm panting hard and having trouble keeping my head above water, too.

"Hang on, little one!" Daisy says as she dives into the water. I watch as Franny then clings onto Daisy's head and holds on while Daisy cuts through the rapids to save her.

I look to the shore to see all the Pawtriots are safe and accounted for. But when I turn back toward the waterfall, I realize it's too late. I'm about to go over the edge. I close my eyes and put my paw over my head to brace for impact.

But, suddenly, I am lifted out of the water by the scruff of my neck.

CHAPTER 5
TEXAS TURKEYS

Location: River
Date: 11MAR21
Time: 1100 hours

I'm dripping wet, completely exhausted, and lying on my back looking up at the blazing sun. Standing silhouetted by the sun is a tall, wiry boxer staring down at me.

The boxer doesn't give me a second to collect myself. He begins barking orders at me and the rest of the Pawtriots.

"On your feet, on your feet!" he shouts.

"Just do what he says," I tell everyone.

"Yeah, that's right. Do exactly as I say. *Form up*, over here. That means 'line up,' in case you civilians weren't tracking!" shouts the boxer.

I knew this guy was military—which branch, I'm not quite sure. But he doesn't seem to be in the mood to answer any questions. We form up into a line as he paces back and forth shaking his head.

"My name is Senior Airman Lindy, or just plain old Lindy to you civilians. And I need answers. Someone care to tell me what in the world the seven of you are doing here? In *my* AO. That's 'area of operations' to you *civvies*. That's short for 'civilians.'"

"We only have two hours . . . ," I begin to say, but Lindy motions his paw at me to stop.

"I'm United States Air Force. I'm high speed and low drag. I track every single plane scheduled to fly over *my* river. So when I see an unapproved air drop land in *my* river, I expect answers. Now, WHO ARE YOU?!" shouts Lindy.

I step up to explain the situation. "My name is—" but Lindy cuts me off.

"Get back in line! You need to focus. I need your nugget in a drool cup. That means pay attention to one thing and one thing only . . . *ME*!" shouts Lindy.

I fall back in line and continue, "I'm Sergeant Rico, and these are the Pawtriots."

Suddenly, I notice Lindy's demeanor changes. He relaxes his stance, and a soft smile spreads across his face. "Well why didn't you just say that? My brother said you'd be landing at E. F. Dunes Air Force Base, not crashing into the river!"

"It's a long story," I say.

"*Oi!* It's actually quite short," says Brick as he thumbs toward Franny. "She accidentally pulled a lever she wasn't supposed to, which sent us flying out the back of the plane."

"Is that right?" says Lindy.

I give Lindy a *north south*. That's Army-talk for "nodding your head when you understand something."

"Can you help get us to to this drop location?" I ask him as I show him Daisy's ransom note.

Lindy stops and thinks for a second and says,

"What business you got there? That place is off limits."

I know Lindy is an ally, but I have to be careful about our *OPSEC*. That's "operational security," and it means you can't go around telling details of your mission to just anyone. My friends in the Navy used to always say "loose lips sink ships."

Lindy can sense my hesitation. "You've got some nerve, Rico. First you make an unapproved land drop into my AO and then you withhold intel!" he shouts.

Lindy's right. He didn't have to help me in the first place. He did it on good faith, and that says a lot about him.

So I continue. "We're on a rescue mission to save her puppies," I say, motioning toward Daisy.

Lindy eyes Daisy up and down. "Rescue mission, huh? And your puppies are in that mine? I find that hard to believe."

"Ditto," says Penny under her breath.

Before Daisy can answer, Brick interjects, "*Oi!* If she said they're down there, then they are down there." Then I watch as Brick gives Daisy a wink as if to suggest "follow my lead."

"And all we're doing is wasting precious time," says Daisy.

"Well, it's not far away, about ten klicks," says Lindy.

"Good, we have to get moving. We're up against a *hard time*," I say. That's Army-talk for a "deadline."

"Rico, we need to rest first," says Penny.

I stand up and walk toward Penny. She meets me halfway and whispers, "This will get worse before it gets better."

I nod my head in agreement, and then I scan the area to make sure it's safe. Establishing security is the first thing you do before letting your unit rest.

"Pawtriots, you have thirty mikes. Catch your breath, get some rest, and then we move out," I tell them.

Lindy starts shaking his head from side to side. "No, no, no. We've got to move. This is hostile territory. Armadillo territory to be exact. And they don't care for trespassers—especially of the canine kind. We have to move out now," he says.

"*Negative*. That's Army-talk for 'no,'" I tell him.

"*Affirmative*. That's Air Force talk for 'yes,'" says Lindy.

"My unit needs to rest," I snap back.

"You're in my AO, and that means *my* jurisdiction, *my* command. What I say goes out here," Lindy says as he brings his big snout right up to mine. "Is that understood, Sergeant?"

I'm about to respond to Lindy, but before I can, I see something strange in the distance.

I quietly whistle to the Pawtriots and motion for them to "look and listen." Penny turns to me and whispers, "What is it?"

I scan the dusty barren landscape more closely, and through the ripples of heat on the horizon I see *it* moving. It looks like rocks, but it's moving. *My mind must be playing tricks on me*, I think. I'm dehydrated and tired, so I rub my eyes and take another look.

Lindy turns around and sees the movement, too. "I think I know what it is. And I know it's no good," he says.

Before I can process what exactly it is that I'm

seeing, a wave of cactus arrows fly through the air and land all around us.

"Ambush!" I howl. And as I say this, I see that the rocks aren't rocks at all.

"Armadillos! Twelve o'clock!" shouts Lindy.

I watch as they race across the dusty plain like a formation of heavily armored desert tanks, hurling their cactus arrows at us as they run.

I want to lead a counterattack, but we're completely exposed. They're closing in on us, and I know I've got to make a tactical decision.

"Pawtriots, *fall back*!" I say.

"This way. Follow me!" shouts Lindy.

We sprint as fast as we can, following Lindy across the desert. But the armadillos are fast, and are quickly surrounding us on all sides.

"What do we do?" Daisy cries out.

"Dig deep and keep running!" I howl back.

Our only chance is to outrun them. This isn't exactly a tactical withdrawal because we can't engage the enemy. It's more like a hasty retreat!

The arrows keep flying, and I realize we're running up against a wall. *Literally.*

They've forced us through the narrow pass of a dried-out canyon. The armadillos have us pinned down and surrounded. In this moment I realize this isn't their first rodeo; they have definitely done this before. They have outsmarted us.

I look around at my fellow Pawtriots and analyze the situation. We have nowhere to run. We're outnumbered and don't stand a chance. I watch as the armadillos snarl with their mouths full of drool as they inch closer to us, just waiting to strike.

"I'm scared, Rico," says Daisy.

I want to tell her that I am, too. I want to tell her that this might be the end of the road for her . . . and for the Pawtriots, but all I can do is watch as the armadillos grunt and squeal frantically. It's as if they can smell their victory . . . and taste it.

"Be brave, Pawtriots," Penny says to us.

The armadillos hold their position as though they are waiting for the order to attack. But from who?

I think about what Kris would do and say in this situation with her back literally up against the wall. *Would she be scared, too?* Then I think about the final Army value: personal courage. It reminds me to face fear, danger, and adversity—no matter the odds.

So I turn to Daisy and the rest of the Pawtriots to lead a counterattack. I stand up tall on my legs and wheel to initiate the charge, when out of the shadows emerges another body.

Suddenly a massive burlap sack flies through the air over the armadillos, landing just before me and the Pawtriots.

CHAPTER 6
DAGR & THE SEVEN POOCHES GANG

Location: Canyon
Date: 11MAR21
Time: 1130 hours

I watch the wild feeding frenzy before me. Like moths drawn to light, the armadillos are completely transfixed with the contents of the burlap sack: a bug buffet filled with hundreds of dead beetles, ants, and termites—all their favorite foods. For a moment, I'm thankful to whoever threw this lifeline our way and that it's not the Pawtriots who are being eaten up.

Then I look beyond the armadillos to see where the burlap sack came from. I see eight nasty-looking mutts staring back at me. I realize now that the armadillos were the least of our problems.

"Oh, sweet boondoggle! That's Dagr," Daisy says in a nervous whisper.

"Hold up just a minute. Did you say 'Dagr'? You don't mean *the* Dagr?" Lindy asks, his voice shaky. This is the first time I've seen him look concerned.

I watch as Dagr and his mutts walk right past the armadillos, thanking them for a mission well done.

"The one and only," says the dog at the center of the pack—a brown and black bull terrier with broad shoulders and an even broader head. His eyes are a cold, pale blue. A twisted mass of scars runs from the top of his head to the bottom of his left eye. He's wearing a tattered tactical vest that is desert brown. He must have been Air Force.

I take one step toward him, and just as my wheel hits the dirt, his seven other mutts step toward me, snarling. The gang is a nasty-looking assortment of big dogs. They've got more drool than brains by the looks of them.

"I've heard a lot about you and that wheel of yours, Rico. The newspapers sure do love their heroes, don't they?" says Dagr with a menacing grin.

"I've heard a lot about you, too, but not in the newspapers. They don't typically cover villains, do they?" I tell him.

"You don't know a thing about me, Pawtriot," scoffs Dagr. I watch as he turns to Daisy, who's scowling at him.

"Nice to see you, too, Daisy," Dagr says with a wink.

"I made it back in time. And I brought the Pawtriots here just like you asked. Now where are my puppies?" asks Daisy.

"Don't play dumb with me, Daisy. It's not a good look on you. I asked you to bring them to the old abandoned mine. And that's about nine *klicks* away. So, we've got some marching to do. Just keep doing what you're told, and the puppies live. If you don't, well . . . they die. All pretty simple," says Dagr.

Then something catches Dagr's eye as he scans the Pawtriots from side to side. He must see Lindy hiding behind Brick.

"*Oi!* Why are you staring at me?" says Brick to Dagr.

"Not you, big pup. I'm looking at that tall, lanky coward behind you," Dagr says as he points at Lindy.

"Listen, Dagr, don't worry about me. I was just about to leave. I've got to get back to our . . . correction . . . I mean *my* unit," Lindy says.

"Negative. You're coming with us. We've got some catching up to do," Dagr scoffs, and looks over at me.

"I should have known the Pawtriots had room for backstabbers and cowards," he says.

Then he turns to his henchmen. "Let's get 'em moving, boys."

Dagr motions and they begin marching us into the unknown.

I can't help but feel a burden of guilt, as I've surrendered all operational control to Dagr and his gang and put the Pawtriots in a sticky situation. Maybe I should have listened more closely to Penny back at the TOC and not accepted this mission.

Still, even in this terrible situation, I remind myself of my Soldier's Creed: *I will never accept defeat.*

I keep marching into the unknown, waiting for an opportunity to turn this mission into a victory and rescue Daisy's pups.

CHAPTER 7
INTO THE MINES

Location: Ridgeline
Date: 11MAR21
Time: 1330 hours

We've been walking for ages, and Dagr hasn't let us stop for water once. And in this part of Texas there aren't many watering holes to begin with. The air is dry, and the ground is dusty and cracked. My paws are covered with blisters and are starting to look like the ground we're walking on.

A few klicks back, Lindy quietly told me that Dagr was in his old unit in the Air Force, but then he got kicked out of the Air Force. I asked him why Dagr was kicked out, but then Dagr got too close to us, so Lindy had to stop talking. Usually if you get kicked out of your unit, it's for something really bad.

Dagr's goons keep poking fun at Brick, who is struggling to keep up.

"Come on, ya big pup. Keep it moving!" Dagr shouts as he pushes Brick along.

"Don't talk to him like that," Penny says, and she pats Brick on the head.

"*Oi!* We've been marching for a bit. I'm just tired is all, and hungry. Real hungry," Brick says.

"Last thing you need is more food, tubby pup. You lack discipline, now keep moving," Dagr says.

I can't stand for bullying—especially when it's about another dog's body. And I'm not about to let somebody outside of *our* unit talk to one of the Pawtriots like that.

"Hey, Dagr. If you have a problem with one of us then you take it up with me," I say as I move in front of Brick and Penny.

"Hold up," Dagr says, and his henchmen stop us in our tracks.

Dagr starts approaching me, but I stand my ground. He presses his big snout against mine. It's full of drool, but I don't back down.

Dagr pushes me and says, "How'd someone as soft as you even make it through boot camp?"

It's like he wants me to fight back, but I'm not

going to react. He's a bully, and this is exactly what he wants. So instead of fighting, I back away. *Some battles aren't worth fighting*, I think.

Naturally, his gang starts howling with laughter. "Coward" and "chicken," they taunt. But I don't let it faze me. I'm focused on keeping my unit safe. I got us into this mess, and I won't do anything to make it worse.

Then Dagr adds even more.

"Captain America here undershot his landing, and his unit's mad at me for the long walk?" he says in disbelief to his goons. "Well, lucky for the chubby bulldog, we're almost there," Dagr says as he points toward a steep trail that cuts across a nearby hill. It twists and winds behind a ridgeline into the unknown.

"Let's move," Dagr says, leading us up the steep trail to the entrance of an abandoned mine shaft at the base of a mountain.

Dagr stops marching and points. Before us is a rotted, splintered timber frame in the side of the mountain. It looks like it used to be the entrance to the old mine shaft. Now it looks like a black hole to nowhere.

I watch as Franny picks up a small stone and throws it through the entrance. I listen as it rattles off the walls as it falls. With each passing second, the echo from the stone is softer, but I can still hear it. Wherever this shaft leads, I know it goes deep into the earth.

"What are we doing in there?" I ask.

"I thought you wanted to save those puppies, hero pup. Don't ask any more questions. Just follow orders," Dagr says.

Before I can even respond, Penny cuts me off. "No! We're not going in without knowing exactly what's down there," she says as she steps up to Dagr.

"Easy now, Miss Pushy," Dagr says, and looks over at me with a grin. "Hey, I thought you were in charge?" he asks mockingly. "Pay attention," he says, motioning for everyone to huddle around him. We all watch as he begins drawing lines in the sand with his paw. It looks like a bunch of random lines at first, but then the lines start taking shape.

"A ssspider?" asks Smithers.

"That's right, snake. This mine ain't exactly abandoned. There's good reason nobody goes down there. The Eight-Legged Killer ain't just some urban legend," Dagr says.

"Yeah, right," Penny says to me under her breath.

"Come on, Dagr. The not-so-itsy-bitsy spider? They weren't doing animal testing down there. That's all made up," says Lindy.

"I've seen it with my own two eyes. Almost lost one of mine last time I was down there," Dagr says, pointing to the scars on his face. "I watched three of my buddies get tangled up in a web faster than you could say 'shoo fly, don't bother me.' And let me tell you, that nasty spider is bigger and badder then you could even imagine. He eats any animal dumb enough to go down there."

Penny does the "tilt." "So technically that makes you dumb, right?"

In an instant, Dagr growls and lunges at Penny, hitting her like a freight train and tackling her to the ground. I rush in with the Pawtriots to help her, but Dagr's goons hold us back.

"Get off of her!" I howl.

"You think you're funny, don't you?" asks Dagr as he presses down hard on Penny.

"Dagr, please! Get off her. I just want my puppies," says Daisy.

Dagr presses down even harder, but eventually

releases Penny. "We're going into that mine. You're all going to help me get that spider, and if I'm feeling nice, Daisy just might get her puppies back. After you, Rico," Dagr says as he points toward the entrance.

As a leader, I'm used to laying out the mission, setting a direction, and executing a plan. But right now we're walking into the darkness, and I'm really starting to second-guess myself and my decision to accept this mission. Still, I remind myself of the Soldier's Creed: *I will always maintain my arms, my equipment, and myself.*

I know I must remain focused and stick with my instincts to lead the Pawtriots out of this mission safely.

CHAPTER 8
WEB SLINGER

Location: Abandoned Mine Shaft
Date: 11MAR21
Time: 1500 hours

I've never been claustrophobic before, but then again, I've never been in an old, abandoned mine shaft like this. It's dark, dirty, and dangerous. The rock walls tighten around us with each step farther into the black abyss. Down here, one thousand feet below the mountain, the earth creaks and groans. Old rusty bolts and rotting timber are the only things stopping us from being crushed. Franny, Smithers, Simon, Penny, Brick, Daisy, and Lindy have entrusted me with their safety, and I intend to keep them safe. This situation is unsettling, but I can't let the Pawtriots see me scared. It will only make them feel worse.

We've been descending into the mine for about an hour now and have yet to come across any spiders, let alone a massive nuclear one.

Then Penny stops and calls me over. She must have found something.

"What is it?" I ask her.

"Old mine carts," she says.

I lean in close and check out the tracks that they're resting on. They appear to be in good working order.

"How much farther?" I ask Dagr.

"Don't tell me you need a break, hero pup. We've got plenty more marching ahead," says Dagr.

"If these tracks lead to where we're going, we can get there faster in these," I say as I point to two mine carts on separate tracks.

Dagr thinks for a second and inspects the mine carts. I can sense his apprehension.

"Dagr, please. My puppies need me," says Daisy.

"Fine, but you," Dagr says as he points at Penny, "you're coming with us."

Penny looks at me and shakes her head as she gets into the mine cart with Dagr and the rest of the Seven Pooches Gang.

"I've got a bad feeling about this," Franny whispers to me.

"Sssame here," Smithers whispers back.

"Come on, stay focused," I say as as the rest of us hop into the other mine cart.

"*Oi!* Franny, why don't you do the honors. You've got a knack for pulling levers," says Brick.

"Real funny," Franny says as she cranks the lever back to release the brake.

We slowly creep forward down the tracks. Our cart is creaky and unstable, but it works, and we begin to pick up speed. I look over to my right and see the other cart moving as well.

We all pick up even more speed. Then we have to bank hard left into an even darker tunnel.

We're moving faster and faster downhill. The carts are screeching against the metal tracks with each bend. It gets louder and louder as we descend farther and deeper into the mine shaft. I can see sparks coming off the sides of the cart from the friction against the tracks.

And then, suddenly, the sound of the carts on the tracks cuts out and I feel weightless. I close my eyes and grip the cart tightly with my paw as we fly over a gap of missing tracks down a steep hill.

I brace for impact.

★ ★ ★

Time: 1515 hours

"*Oi!* I did not sign up for this, Rico!" Brick says as we safely land on the other side. The tracks below us flatten out and we come to a slow stop.

"Lots of tasty treats for you back at the TOC, I promise," I tell him.

"Where's Penny?" Daisy asks.

It's pitch black, so I have no idea. All I hear is what sounds like someone tinkering with a switch. Lots of clinking and clanging.

"Lindy, is that you?" I ask.

"No, it's me and Simon," says Franny.

"What are you two tinkering with?" I ask them.

Before they can respond, I hear a humming *buzz* that grows louder. Then there's a loud *POP* and a single light flashes on, then another and another.

I watch as, one by one, more lights turn on until the entire area is illuminated. I quickly scan my surroundings to see that we're on the lower level of a massive man-made cavern. In the distance I see an abandoned laboratory with lab equipment: beakers, microscopes, and a strange, massive contraption that I've never seen before in my life. Whoever left this place last, left here in a hurry.

"Where in the dickens are we?" asks Daisy.

"Beats me," I tell her.

"I know," Lindy says, his voice shaky. We all turn to him. "They said this place didn't exist. Back in the Air Force, dogs would talk about this place. I always assumed it was straight from the rumor mill, an urban legend like Bigfoot. Just some big joke," he says.

"Please tell me this is just a joke," Brick chimes in quickly.

"Afraid not, friend. This is Area 6," says Lindy.

"What is *that*?" Brick asks.

"A top-secret US government testing facility," Lindy replies.

"Tesssting for what?" asks Smithers.

"Animals . . . *nuclear* animals," Lindy says as he scans the area.

"Daisy, this is where he has your puppies?" I ask with concern.

Daisy begins to open her mouth to speak, but she closes it before answering. Something isn't right, I can sense it. I watch her look up to the second level to where Dagr, Penny, and the rest of the Seven Pooches Gang are.

"Go on, Daisy, tell him the *truth*," says Dagr.

All of a sudden, Penny lurches forward. "Rico, it's a—"

But before she can finish, two of the gang members grab her and cover her mouth.

"Shut her up, would you?" says Dagr to his henchmen.

"What's going on, Daisy? What's this all about?" I ask.

x

61

Daisy shakes her head at Dagr. "I won't," she says.

"Just tell us where her puppies are, Dagr!" I howl.

Dagr steps forward. "You still don't get it, do you?"

I stare blankly at Dagr and back at Penny, whose mouth is still being covered by the two nasty mutts.

"You really are as dumb as you look, hero pup. Can't you see? There ain't no puppies here!" Dagr says, letting out a devious laugh.

"Let me go! I did what you asked, Dagr. Just let me go see my puppies now," says Daisy.

I don't know what to say or what to think. All I know is Penny was right: This golden isn't friendly. Daisy led us right into a Texas-size trap at the bottom of this abandoned mine. And there's no way out.

CHAPTER 9
A TAIL OF REVENGE

Location: Area 6
Date: 11MAR21
Time: 1530 hours

"What's this all about, Dagr? What do you want from me? What do you want from the Pawtriots?" I ask him.

He howls out in laughter, and the rest of his seven nasty mutts join in. Once Dagr settles down, he asks, "Does the name Chaps mean anything to you?" And before I can get a word out, he continues, "Sergeant First Class Chaps, that is. Well that name means a whole lot to me. Chaps and I went way back. We knew each other since we were just little puppy dogs. We were at the Academy together, we were commissioned together, and we did our tours of duty together. He was the top Army dog and I was top of the Air Force. We were quite the dynamic duo."

"Chaps would never be friends with a nasty dog like you," I say.

"Oh, yes he would. We were best friends. But on our third tour, my best friend, my brother in arms, betrayed me. He stabbed me right in the back."

"You must have done something really bad then. Chaps was the most loyal dog I have ever met," I say.

"Loyal?!" Dagr snaps back at me. "He sided with some worthless villagers over me! We were in the business of following orders and saving lives, and I was just following orders!"

"What does any of this have to do with me and the Pawtriots?" I ask.

"It's been seven years since Chaps got me kicked out of the Air Force. And for seven long years I've sworn revenge. He tried to make it right, but I wouldn't have it. He took everything from me, and while he was wasting time with apologies, I was planning out my revenge. I was chasing him across this country. I guess that means I was chasing you, too," says Dagr as he points to Franny and Smithers. "I got word he was in DC, so I sent three of my best dogs to get him and bring him back here."

"It wasss you! Thossse were *your* nasssty dogsss chasssing us!" says Smithers.

"You're the reason Chaps got caught by the Snatchers!" says Franny.

"I lost three of my best dogs, my career, my life! Don't talk to me about loss," shouts Dagr.

"Dagr, just think about this," I say.

"Oh, I've thought plenty. For seven years, to be exact. And every day and night I thought about how I would exact my revenge on Chaps, to take away something important to him, to take away *his* life. And then he got mixed up with you and your no-good Pawtriots. It was supposed to be *me* who took him down, not some wicked Beast in the depths of the sewers. *Me!*"

"Dagr, it doesn't have to end like this," I say.

"Oh yes it does, Rico. Look at you! You're wearing Chaps's wheel. A piece of him still roams this earth. I want to make sure there isn't a single trace of that backstabbing traitor!"

I watch as one of the dogs walks over to the catwalk leading up to the second level and kicks it off its hinges, sending it crashing down to the depths below. I realize that was our only way out.

Dagr turns and motions to his gang. At his signal, they forcefully grab Penny.

"Get your filthy paws off of me! Rico, help!" Penny shouts as they drag her away and slip into the darkness.

"Dagr, wait! What about my puppies?!" Daisy howls.

Dagr turns back around and a big grin stretches across his face. "Don't worry. They'll fit right in with my gang. And besides, y'all have bigger problems!" Dagr shouts, pointing behind us to a dark tunnel in the side of the cave.

I quickly turn around and look but can't see anything except for darkness. All I hear is a bubbling *hiss* coming from inside the hole.

Then, out of the shadows, a creature emerges.

"You walked us right into a trap," Franny says, scowling at Daisy.

"Backsssstabber," says Smithers.

"I'm so sorry, y'all," Daisy says with her tail between her legs.

We're all frozen. Gripped with fear and curiosity as to what this hideous creature's next move will be. The massive spider hisses and roars. Its breath sends Franny tumbling back, and the foul smell nearly makes me gag.

"Get ready for evasive maneuvers, Pawtriots. This eight-legged nuclear freak looks fast," whispers Lindy.

"You mean ssscatter?" Smithers whispers back.

"I think he means run for dear life," Daisy says nervously.

I study its movements quickly to get a sense of the enemy before me. I need to come up with a tactical strategy, and fast. I look down at my wheel and wonder if perhaps it has multiple uses.

The nuclear spider hisses at me, and I know it's about ready to strike.

"Hold, Pawtriots, steady now. Wait for it to make its move," I say as I slowly unhinge my wheel, removing it from my body. I hold it above my head and swing it in the air from side to side like a bullfighter with his red cape.

"It's working," I say quietly to the Pawtriots.

The motion is distracting the spider, and now I know exactly how to get us out of here. Its greatest strength may be its biggest weakness.

"You just gonna wave at the thing?" says Lindy.

"No. Can you help me run?" I ask.

I keep waving my wheel, enticing the spider more and more, until suddenly . . .

"Pawtriots, run!" I howl.

I lean on Lindy and the Pawtriots scatter, sprinting away in different directions, but the spider is intent on chasing me. It's fixated on my wheel leg, and that's the plan. Lindy helps me weave over and under obstacles as the spider shoots its webbing—a jet stream of sticky liquid silk—at us.

We scramble from side to side and barely manage to avoid being hit. This spider is big and fast, but Lindy and I are small enough to dodge in and out of spaces it can't.

"What's the plan, Rico?" shouts Lindy.

"First, help me get my wheel back on, then we need to get to the second level," I howl back. "We need to save Penny!"

Lindy helps me put my wheel back on as we lumber across the broken catwalks. The spider chases us, giving the other Pawtriots an opening to maneuver safely up to the second level using the cobweb rope the spider created by shooting its webbing at me. We dodge a few more webbings and look back over our shoulders to see the spider barreling down on us.

"Get up here, Rico!" shouts Franny from the second level.

"Make hassste!" says Smithers.

"Coming right up!" I say to the Pawtriots as Lindy and I race up the webbing, and then—*WHAM*—the spider nails me with a shot of its web, sending me crashing down onto the catwalk below.

I'm covered in its sticky web. I'm slow to get up and my hind leg is throbbing, but I need to push through the pain. I start crawling back up to safety on the second level.

"Double-time, Rico!" Lindy shouts out to me.

"*Oi!* Behind you!" Brick hollers.

I don't even turn around to look, there's no

time. I know that massive nuclear spider is right on my tail. I keep crawling as fast as I can across the grated catwalk. Below me is at least a twenty-foot drop to the bottom.

I weave in and out of the nooks and crannies of the mine as I make my way up to Lindy, who has his paws stretched out wide for me.

"Jump, Rico!"

Easier said than done, I think to myself as I stand on all fours—my wheel is locked and loaded. I take three steps back to get a running start.

"Hooah!" I call out as I land safely on the second level where the rest of the Pawtriots are.

Then the massive spider shoots out another jet stream of webbing to latch onto the railing on the second level. We all watch as it begins climbing up the webbing, making its way toward us, until—SNAP—the massive spider is too big and too heavy to be held by its own unfinished web. Then, it falls onto the twisted metal of broken catwalks below.

"Let's keep moving, Pawtriots," I say, and we begin our ascent out of the depths of the abandoned mine.

CHAPTER 10
TRUTH BE TOLD

Location: Valley
Date: 11MAR21
Time: 1830 hours

We can finally breathe fresh air.

The sky is an awesome mix of purple with orange streaks. The sun looks enormous as it sets on the horizon, but in the distance is a terrible formation of dark clouds. A storm is rolling in. All I want to do is lie down and rest, but I can't. Dagr and his no-good gang of pooches have Penny, and I have no idea where they've taken her or what they want with her.

"Catch your breath, Pawtriots. We're moving out in two mikes," I say.

I look over at Franny, who is studying the ground. "I think I see paw prints. Heading south," she says.

"Lindy, do you have any idea where they would take her?" I ask.

Lindy pauses to think for a second and then his eyes light up. "His old hideout! Dagr had this spot on the other side of the border. He took me there one time. He would go there when he needed to clear his mind. I can only imagine what he does there now," says Lindy.

"He must have my puppies there, too! We have to hurry!" Daisy cries out.

"You're not coming with us, Daisy. We're going to save Penny and your puppies. You can meet us at the Air Force base later. We will bring your puppies there," I say.

"I'm coming, Rico! I can help. Those puppies need their mama," Daisy says.

"Why should we trust you? You got us into this mess! They have Penny!" I shout.

"Rico, I should have told y'all the truth. I know what happened is my fault. I'm sorry, but I had no choice!" says Daisy.

"Everyone hasss a choice, and you chossse to lie," says Smithers as Simon shoos Daisy away.

"I told you. There is no choice with Dagr. He and his gang do what they want, where they want, to whomever they want! Those puppies are my everything, and I am willing to do anything for them," says Daisy.

The Pawtriots have their eyes on me, waiting for me to make a decision.

"Let me help, please," says Daisy.

"Forget her, Rico. She can't be trusted," says Franny.

"I know what Daisy did was wrong. She lied to us and put us all in harm's way. But her back was against a wall, and she made a tough choice in order to save her puppies. The end justifies the means," I say.

"But, Rico—" Franny cuts in.

"But what? Wouldn't you have done the same? We need to forgive Daisy and move on. One of our fellow Pawtriots is missing, and we can't leave a fallen comrade behind. Every second we waste is a second too long."

Lindy chimes in, "He's right. We need to put our differences aside and let bygones be bygones.

Dagr is former Air Force, so he'll be prepared and ready to try and stop us."

"Lindy, do you have any intel on this place?" I ask.

"Affirmative," he says. "I can get us in. But it's getting across the border that's going to be the hard part."

CHAPTER 11
RESCUE MISSION

Location: US–Mexico Border
Date: 11MAR21
Time: 2200 hours

It's pouring rain, and dark clouds roll across the sky.

"See that culvert over there, ten o'clock, across the border?" asks Lindy as he points to a three-foot-wide pipe that cuts through a mound of dirt and concrete one hundred yards away.

I scan the area and locate the culvert. "I've got *eyes on it.*" I tell Lindy. That's Army-talk for "I can see what you're pointing out."

"Dagr's hideout is in there," says Lindy.

"I'll start chewing a hole in the fence," says Franny.

"Negative, it will set off the alarm. We have to sneak through with the cars," says Lindy.

"And how do you propossse we do that?" says Smithers.

Simon tugs on my shoulder and motions that he has an idea and a plan to get across. I'm having a hard time interpreting his hand and arm signals, but I think I understand. Before I can even relay Simon's plan to the rest of the Pawtriots, he bolts.

"Where's he going?" Franny asks.

"He'sss officially gone rogue," Smithers says.

We all watch in amazement as Simon weaves in and out of traffic, stopping only when a border patrol agent gets too close. Simon remains perfectly still for a few seconds and then, in an instant, he bolts again, scurrying under and hopping over cars.

"Well that's one way to get across the border!" says Lindy.

Simon makes his way up to the guard's tower, where he has a perfect vantage point of all the border patrol agents.

"Listen up, Pawtriots," I say. "Here's the plan. Keep your eyes on Simon. When he motions to 'move,' we move. When he motions to 'stop,' we stop. Don't think, just act and follow his hand and arm signals."

Simon waves us on, and we all move forward as fast as we can. Then he motions for us to "stop." We hold our position as a border patrol agent and his dog search a minivan in front of us. The dog has her nose low to the ground and is sniffing fast. She's a brown lab and looks very determined. Suddenly, she starts barking!

"She's got our scent," whispers Franny.

I look up at Simon, but he's still got us in a *hold* position, meaning "don't move." The minivan starts to slowly roll forward, exposing us. Quickly, Simon motions for us to "go-go-go!"

We race forward and are almost across the

border when Simon suddenly motions for us to "stop." We tuck up against the minivan, and I scan the area. The border patrol agent and his dog are right across from us. The brown lab spots us. She's alarmed and confused. She starts howling and barking, alerting the border agents.

Simon motions for us to "go," and we all bolt.

We race past some busy guards, get across the border, and tumble down a ridge into a ditch that leads to the culvert.

We enter the tunnel, moving fast. The heavy rain is sending rushing water filled with trash and debris through the pipe. The water rages against the damp stone walls, but at least we can see in here. The walls are lined with dim utility lights.

We follow Lindy and pass by a couple of tunnel shafts. Then he banks left and leads us down some stairs that wind and twist even farther underground until we arrive at a set of metal bars that look down into a vast cavern-like room. I see a grate in the middle with water running under it. The walls are covered in vines and moss and the floors are piled with trash.

From up here I can see Penny, who is in the middle of the room and chained to the floor along with Daisy's three puppies. I can hear Dagr and his gang poking fun at Penny.

"Be very quiet," I say. "Wait for the word and then we strike."

"What's the word?" Franny asks.

"You'll know it when I say it," I tell them as we listen in to Dagr taunting Penny below us.

CHAPTER 12
SECOND CHANCES

Location: Dagr's Hideout
Date: 11MAR21
Time: 2230 hours

We all watch silently while Dagr enters the cage and approaches Penny. "Please, Dagr! Let me go," Penny shouts as she jerks at the puppies' chains. "At least let these poor puppies free."

"Now why would I do that? These puppies are my new recruits. I need you to take care of them for the time being," he says.

I watch as Dagr pulls out a key from a cord around his neck.

I turn to the Pawtriots and howl out, "*Hooah!*" and I jump down into the middle of the room.

The rest of the Pawtriots follow, and we form a circle around Penny.

"Impossible! We left you for dead," says Dagr.

"Where there's a will, there's a way," I tell him.

The Seven Pooches Gang slowly circles around us, as water begins to fill the room.

"Hero pup and his Pawtriots miraculously escape that good-for-nothing spider. Well, if you want something done right, you gotta do it yourself," says Dagr.

We're surrounded but evenly matched. Two opposing forces waiting to strike.

"Just let Penny go," I say.

"Not a chance," says Dagr.

"It's never too late to do what's right," I say.

"The time for being good has passed, hero pup," says Dagr.

I realize that I can't change Dagr's mind. He and his gang are itching for a fight. The Pawtriots are ready to do whatever it takes to save Penny, but I think I can stop this battle before it starts. Selfless service is one of the Army values and it reminds me to put the safety of my unit before my own.

"Let's settle this, Dagr. You and me. Dog versus dog," I say.

"I'll gladly destroy you first and then I'll destroy

your entire unit," says Dagr.

I look at the Pawtriots and quietly say, "For Chaps," and then I turn and charge at Dagr. Without hesitating, he snarls and charges at me. We both leap forward at each other and collide hard in midair.

We fall to the ground fighting fiercely, locked in a grapple, each struggling to gain the upper paw. I manage to pin Dagr to the ground, but I let my right ear get too close to his mouth.

I let out a loud howl as Dagr bites down on my ear.

"You're no match for me," Dagr says as he spits my blood out of his mouth. We both spring to our feet and begin circling each other as more water pours and floods into the room.

I charge at Dagr and launch him backward. He loses his footing on the slippery floor and crashes to the ground. He's slow to his feet. His menacing confidence starts to waiver, so I pounce on top of him and use my wheel leg to hold him down. The water starts to rise past his neck. I don't want him to drown, so I let him go.

"Enough! It's over!" I shout as Dagr slowly rises to his feet and takes the key to their chains off its cord and holds it in his mouth. Dagr lowers his head and slowly steps toward me. He's helpless, defeated.

"You're doing the right thing," I tell him.

I'm slowly reaching for the key when Dagr looks up and stares right into my eyes. I watch as his facial expression transforms in an instant from defeated to devious. I quickly reach for the key and almost have it in my mouth when Dagr drops it through the grate below, letting the rushing water carry it away.

"No!" I howl.

"Move out, boys! This place is going to flood," Dagr says, and his gang makes their way up a rope ladder and out through a vent.

"Cowards!" shouts Penny from inside the cage.

"You see, Penny, life is war!" Dagr says as he pulls the rope ladder up with him. "I can deal with the harsh realities. I never wanted praise and I didn't want medals. What I *do* want is to survive! That's what Chaps and all you no-good Pawtriots could never understand. Moral superiority doesn't keep you alive."

On his way out he bangs on one of the pipes, bursting it and sending even more water into the already flooding room.

I need to act quickly and come up with an escape plan. There's a tunnel in the corner of the room, but I have no idea where it leads.

"Franny, can you get the lock on their chains open?" I ask.

"I'm on it," says Franny as she begins to tinker with the lock. "I need something small and pointy to pick this lock!" she shouts.

"Search the trash!" I howl. The Pawtriots start

rummaging through the junk and debris as I rip bags of trash open with my teeth and try not to breathe in the smell. It's disgusting, but we're running out of time. I'm lifting my head up to suck in some fresh air when I see Simon take a swan dive into the garbage. He disappears into the pile and comes out holding a paper clip. He straightens the clip out and races it over to Franny.

"Bingo!" she says.

Franny works the paper clip into the lock's keyhole as water begins to rise into the room. Penny lifts the little puppies onto her back to keep their heads above water.

"Hurry, Franny!" howls Daisy.

"Got it!" shouts Franny as the lock pops open, freeing Penny and the pups.

Penny rushes over to Daisy with the puppies on her back.

"My puppies!" cries Daisy as she hugs and kisses them all. "Thank you, Penny!" she says.

"Don't mention it," says Penny.

"Hold your breath, Pawtriots!" I shout when the room is nearly filled with water. "The tunnel is our only way out. Let's go!"

We file one by one into the tunnel, the rushing water carrying us quickly. We have no idea where it leads, but it's our only option. I'm having trouble keeping my head above water, when suddenly . . .

"Mudslide!" Lindy calls out.

It feels like the entire earth below me is falling as we're sucked through the tunnel and dumped into a bay. If my bearings are correct, I'd say we are headed right into the Gulf of Mexico.

The winds are raging, the sea is swelling, and splintered fallen trees are everywhere. We manage to stay together and latch onto a massive floating logs with branches, using it as a flotation device to navigate the muddy waters.

"Eyes to the front, everyone. We're not out of this yet!" shouts Lindy.

Massive pieces of debris slam against our makeshift flotilla as we bank left and right at the mercy of the mudslide.

I look up and see Dagr and the Seven Pooches Gang floating on top of a small tree branch. There isn't enough room for all of them, and they start fighting among themselves for space on their splintered log. One by one they start falling into the muddy water, vanishing before our eyes, until it's just Dagr floating through the swirling mud alone.

He's heading right for a partially submerged building and is about to crash. I should be thinking *good riddance*, but I can't help myself from feeling sorry for him.

"Dagr, look out!" I howl.

Dagr looks up and scans the situation, as if looking for a way out. But he knows his time is up. He looks over at me and gives me a defiant salute just as he slams into the building and disappears into the muddy water.

For a moment, I breathe with relief.

The good news is Dagr and the Seven Pooches Gang are gone. They won't be able to terrorize the world anymore.

The bad news is that we're drifting farther out to sea with no food, no water, and no plan.

CHAPTER 13
COME SAIL AWAY

Location: Lost at Sea
Date: 14MAR21
Time: 2345 hours

It's been almost three days since we were swept out into the Gulf of Mexico.

The sea has calmed down since the storm, but it looks like another is brewing ahead. Everyone is asleep except Simon. He has barely slept a wink since we've been out here. Simon says these waters are dangerous and it's not just the waves and the sharks. He says that pirate ships roam the sea. Thankfully we haven't seen any yet. He says he once spent time at a zoo not too far from here. I don't know how he can tell where he is. We're surrounded by ocean—the land vanished from view quickly—but maybe he just senses it.

While Simon plays sentry, I've been trying to

flag down one of the birds that keeps buzzing past us. I need to get a message home. Everyone at the TOC is probably wondering how we're doing. But every time I get close to one of the birds, they just fly away.

I'm trying to keep everyone's spirits high even though our situation looks grim. We have no food, no drinkable water, and there's no land in sight. But like we said back in the Army, *false motivation is better than no motivation.*

Date: 15MAR21
Time: 0230 hours

A storm has been raging all night, and even I'm having trouble staying positive. Our makeshift floating device is falling apart, and it's getting harder and harder to stay afloat.

I manage to catch the attention of a young seagull, who says she'll take my message to DC. I know it might be pointless, but I don't want anyone to think I've given up hope—I pass the message to the seagull:

SitRep (Situation Report)
15 MAR 21
The Pawtriots

Coordinates unknown.
We are effectively lost at sea.
Our class 1 (food and water) is gone.

Overall mission SUCCESS:
Dag'r and the seven Pooches gang
have been stopped.
We have added friendly forces to
our ranks. Lindy, Daisy, and her pups.

Every effort is being made to RTB
(Return to Base)
All hope is not lost.
Stand by for further instructions.

—Sergeant "Rico" Ricochet

The seagull flies away as lightning shoots from the sky and strikes the ocean.

I quickly realize just how dangerous this situation is now.

"Get low!" I shout as a wall of rain sweeps over us and the ocean begins to roll. The thunder is deafening. Lightning flashes burst through the rain. Some of the waves are as high as houses. Our makeshift flotation device rides up one side, then plunges down the next. All we can do is hold on.

I stare out to sea, searching for someone or something to help.

Then I see two faint lights appear way off in the distance, close together and growing brighter.

Simon signals to me, "Pirates!"

"Pawtriots, prepare to defend yourselves!" I howl.

They race toward us. One ship is ahead of the other. I watch as it cuts through the waves, speeding closer and closer to us. The light on the front of the ship is pointed directly at us.

I stand tall on the edge of the floating log. The light shines directly into my eyes, and for a moment I can't see. Then the light turns off.

I squint and adjust my eyes. I realize that these aren't pirate ships.

"It's the US Coast Guard!" I howl.

The rest of the Pawtriots cheer and howl. And for a moment, we forget about the treacherous situation we are in while the Coast Guard nears. Then, as I look up at the storm raging above me, I worry that even with the help of the Coast Guard, we may not be able to make it back to Washington, DC, back to the TOC, and back home to see the rest of the Pawtriots. Only time will tell . . .